# Hole in the ZOO

## Chloë and Mick Inkpen

**M**onday morning
at Number 2.
Who's coming through
the hole in the . . .

Four stripey things . . .

...and a **spotty one too!**

It ran round the bedroom
and pounced on my shoe.
Then it got into bed
with Ellie and Boo!

This is Ellie

This is Boo

Tuesday evening
at Number 2.
Who's coming through
the hole in the . . .

Ten jumpy frogs...

...and a small **kangaroo!**

**W**ednesday bathtime
at Number 2.
Who's coming through
the hole in the . . .

Flamingos and penguins . . .

...and a **pelican** too!

**22** animals
(not counting Boo).

And they all
made a mess
with the soap
and shampoo!

Thursday lunchtime
at Number 2.
Who's coming through
the hole in the . . .

Some bright orange monkeys . . .

. . . and a man from the **ZOO**!

He told them all off
and sent them back through.

All day Friday at Number 2
we waited and waited
but nothing came through.
Nothing came through
the hole in the . . .

except for a tortoise . . .

. .and that did a poo. (And I'm not even sure that it came from the zoo.)

**S**aturday morning
at Number 2.
Still nothing through
the hole in the...

# ZOO.

Nothing to do.
Nothing to do.
Absolutely nothing to do.

**S**aturday midnight
at Number 2 . . .

. . .where are you going,
Ellie and Boo?

Sunday morning
at Number 2.
Ellie is missing.
And so is Boo!

What shall we do?
What shall we do?
Where have you gone to,
Ellie and Boo?

Harrrrumph!

Out in the garden
at Number 2.
Here they are
at the hole in the . . .

Harrrumph!

o!

Ellie and Boo
and a **big bottom** too!

Who's squeezing through?
Who's squeezing through?

Can you guess who?
(Boo is the clue.)

# An elephant!

With a **baby** like Boo!
And one of the monkeys,
and two cockatoos . . .